Dedicated to my dear, God-fearing grandfathers, Littrel Josh Thomas and Lynn Brebner Bowles. Thank you for always inspiring me, and making me want to be a better man.

ADINA PUBLISHING

MASCOT BOOKS

www.mascotbooks.com

Mat With Only One t

©2016 Jeff Thomas. All Rights Reserved. No part of this publication may be reproduced, stored in a retrieval system or transmitted in any form by any means electronic, mechanical, or photocopying, recording or otherwise without the permission of the author.

For more information, please contact:
Mascot Books
560 Herndon Parkway #120
Herndon, VA 20170
info@mascotbooks.com

Adina Publishing
P.O. Box 791
Flagstaff, AZ 86002
www.adinapublishing.com

Library of Congress Control Number: 2016907906

CPSIA Code: PRT1016B
ISBN: 978-1-63177-596-3

Printed in the United States

Matt
with only one t

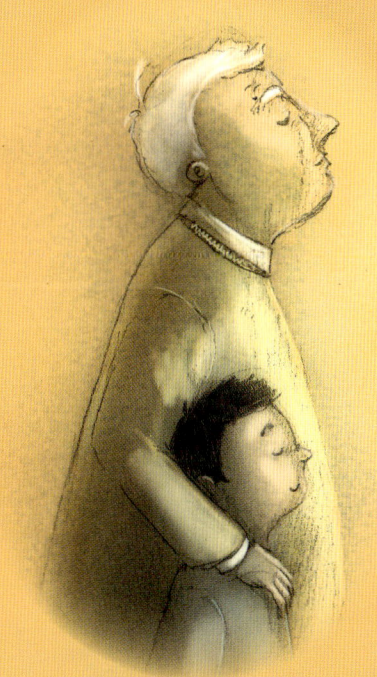

by Jeff Thomas

Illustrated by Andrea Alemanno

My name is Mat, with only one t.
I gave away my other t
to someone dear to me.

Where should I start?
I'll start with my heart.
I learned from the start
that my heart's the best part.

You see, when I was just three,
my grandpa taught me
the best gifts in life
are the gifts that are free.

At night after playing with
    Grandpa all day,
he would rock me to sleep
    and these words he did say,

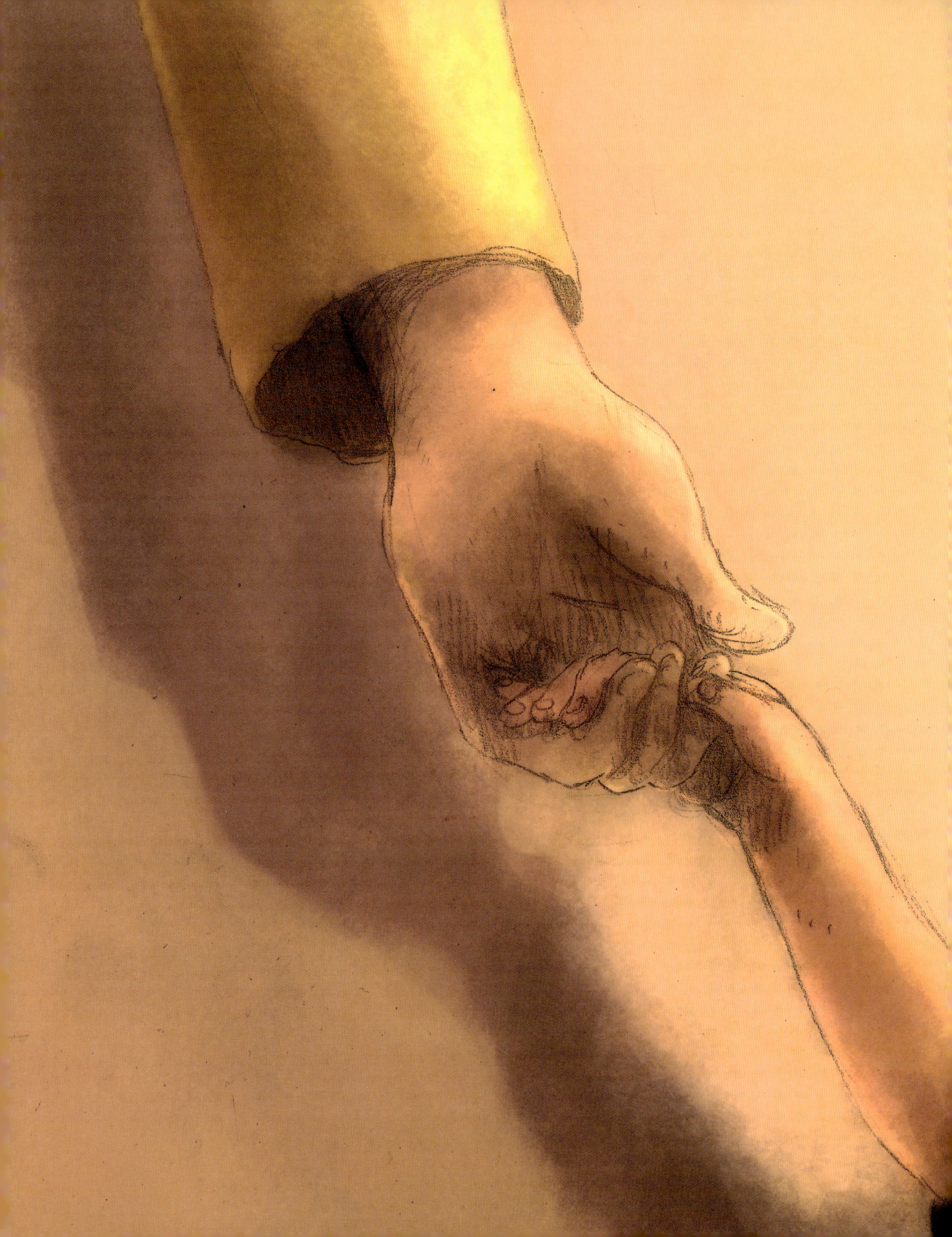

"Give with a smile
and give from your heart,
and your gift will keep giving
even when you're apart."

He would talk about life
and places to see,
and as I faded to sleep,
he'd again say to me,

"Give with a smile
and give from your heart,
and your gift will keep giving
even when you're apart."

My grandpa would tell me
　　to reach for the stars
and to treat people equally,
　　like they're family of ours.

"Stand up for your neighbor,
　　don't be scared to speak,
and offer your hand,
　　especially to the weak."

So as the day ended
　　and the sun finally set,
Grandpa sat me down
　　and said, "Son, please don't forget…"

"To give with a smile
and give from your heart,
and your gift will keep giving
even when you're apart."

Like I told you at first,
    I'm Mat with only one t.
I gave away my other t
    to someone dear to me.

God soon needed Grandpa,
    so He called him away
to go up to Heaven and
brighten His day.

I saw Grandpa that night
   as he rested in bed.
I told him stories
   then kissed his soft head.

"I know you must go,
   and it hurts me so much."
He put his hand on mine,
   and I felt his sweet touch.

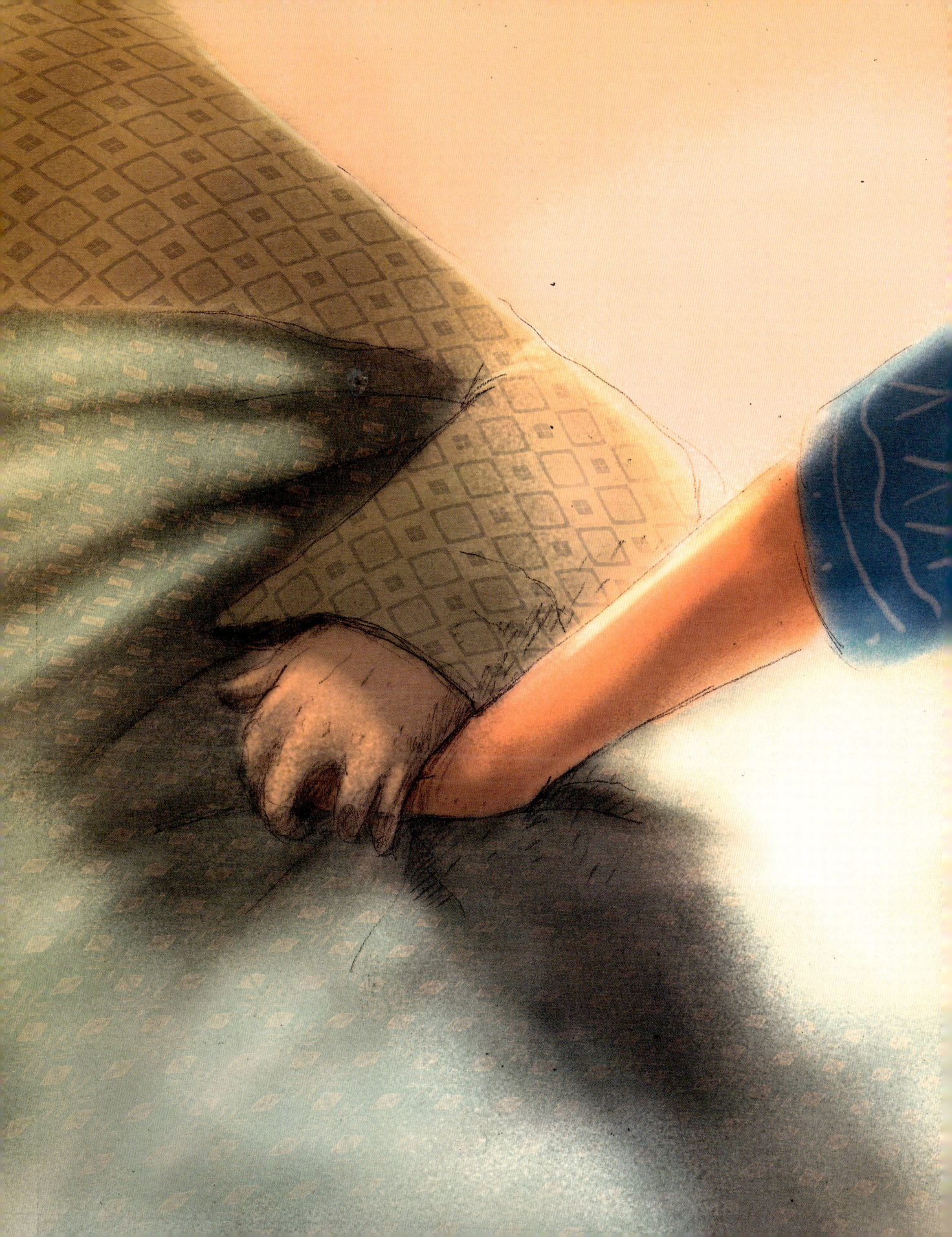

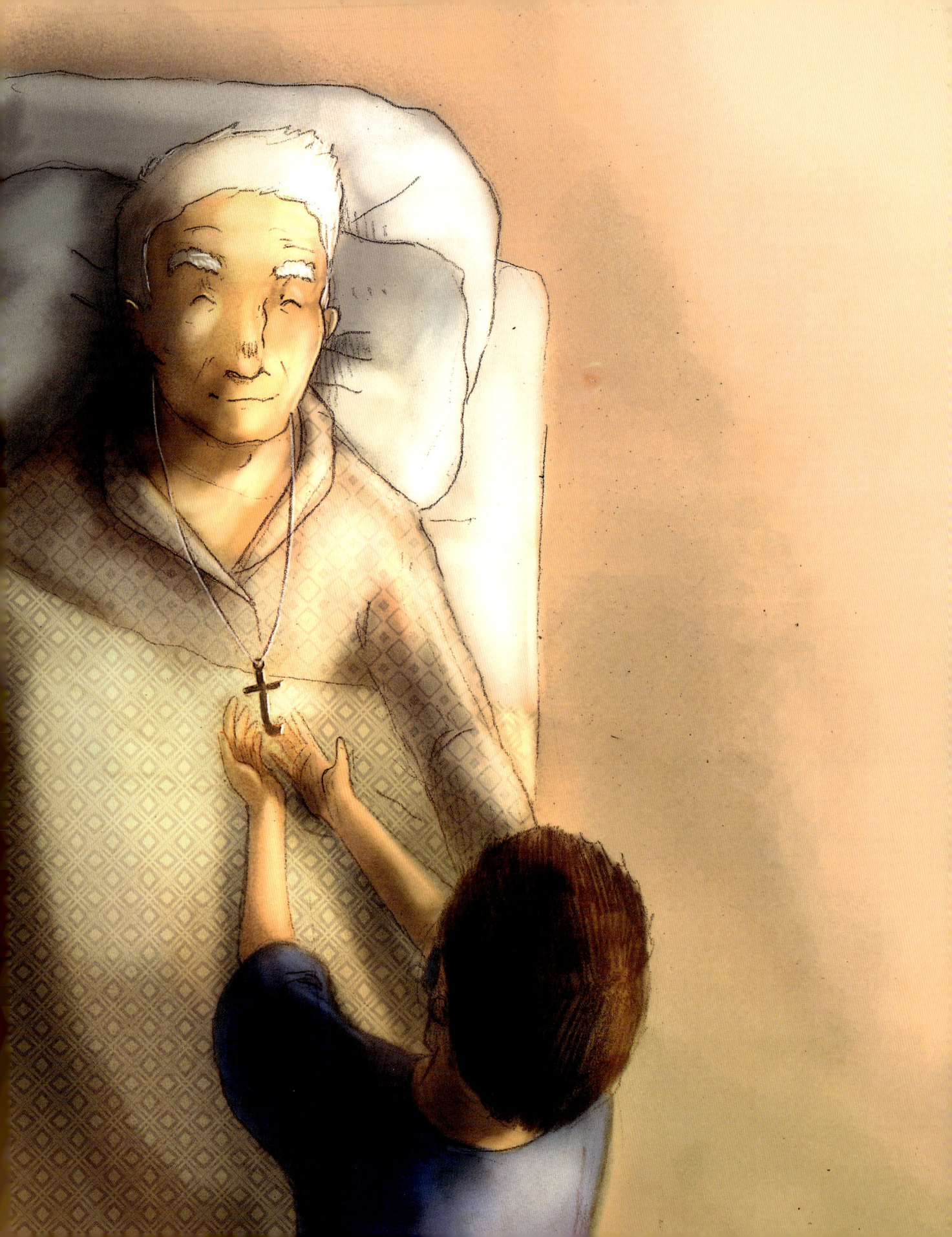

I said, "I have you a gift,
   and this gift is from me."
Then I said these great words
  a wise man once told me.

"I give with a smile
    this gift from my heart—
a t from my name,
    while we're briefly apart.

So please take this t
    and please hold it tight.
Please take it, Grandpa,
    with you to Heaven tonight."

About the Author

Jeff Thomas was inspired to write *Mat With Only One t* because of the close relationships he had with both of his grandfathers while growing up in Texas. Jeff is a graduate of Baylor University in Waco, Texas, and currently lives in Central Illinois with his wife, Sarah, and their three children, Makenzie, Tanner, and Tenley.

ADINA PUBLISHING

Adina Publishing is devoted to publishing inspirational stories for children and adults. The name derives from Adina Schrag, a family matriarch who had an elementary school education but wrote her memoir before she passed away at age 93 and encouraged her children, grandchildren, and great grandchildren to do the same. Several have accepted that challenge. She lived an active, full, and faith-filled life. Her spirit is a fitting tribute to books that her namesake publishing house shares with the world.

Contact Adina Publishing for media and retail inquiries as well as your book ideas at:

Adina Publishing
P.O. Box 791
Flagstaff, AZ 86002
(928) 679-5060

Myles.Schrag@adinapublishing.com | www.AdinaPublishing.com

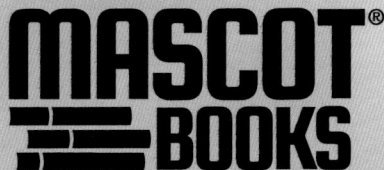

Have a book idea?
Contact us at:

Mascot Books
560 Herndon Parkway
Suite 120
Herndon, VA 20170

info@mascotbooks.com | www.mascotbooks.com